IN LOVING MEMORY OF PAT

SIMON & SCHUSTER BOOKS FOR YOUNG READERS
An imprint of Simon & Schuster Children's Publishing Division
1230 Avenue of the Americas, New York, New York 10020
© 2021 by Jessie Sima
Book design by Lizzy Bromley © 2021 by Simon & Schuster, Inc.
All rights reserved, including the right of reproduction in whole or in part in any form.
SIMON & SCHUSTER BOOKS FOR YOUNG READERS
and related marks are trademarks of Simon & Schuster, Inc.
For information about special discounts for bulk purchases, please contact Simon & Schuster
Special Sales at 1-866-506-1949 or business@simonandschuster.com.
The Simon & Schuster Speakers Bureau can bring authors to your live event.
For more information or to book an event, contact the Simon & Schuster Speakers
Bureau at 1-866-248-3049 or visit our website at www.simonspeakers.com.
The text for this book was set in Baskerville.
The illustrations for this book were rendered in Photoshop.
Manufactured in China • 0421 SCP • First Edition
2 4 6 8 10 9 7 5 3 1
Library of Congress Cataloging-in-Publication Data
Names: Sima, Jessie, author, illustrator. • Title: Hardly haunted / Jessie Sima.
Description: First edition. | New York : Simon & Schuster Books for Young Readers, [2021]
| Audience: Ages 4-8. | Audience: Grades K-1. | Summary: When a house believes she is
haunted, she tries everything in her power to stop it in order to get people to move in—until she
realizes that she is fine just the way she is.
Identifiers: LCCN 2020034444 (print) | LCCN 2020034445 (eBook)
ISBN 9781534441705 (hardcover) | ISBN 9781534441712 (eBook)
Subjects: CYAC: Haunted houses—Fiction.
Classification: LCC PZ7.1.S548 Im 2021 (print) | LCC PZ7.1.S548 (eBook) | DDC [E]—dc23
LC record available at https://lccn.loc.gov/2020034444
LC eBook record available at https://lccn.loc.gov/2020034445

HARDLY
HAUNTED

JESSIE SIMA

Simon & Schuster Books for Young Readers
New York London Toronto Sydney New Delhi

There was a house on a hill,
and that house was worried.

"I'm a house," thought the house.
"People are supposed to live in me."
But no one did.

Which was pretty suspicious.

"I think . . . ," thought the house,

"I might be . . ."

FOR
SALE

The house did not *want* to be haunted.
Who would want to live in a haunted house?

"If I'm on my very best behavior," she thought, "maybe no one will notice how spooky I am."

"There's no hiding that I'm dusty,
and full of cobwebs."

"But if I hold still, maybe my doors won't . . ."

"And if I keep quiet,
maybe my stairs won't . . ."

"This isn't working," she thought.
"I'll have to try harder."

The house held her breath.

She kept VERY still.

And VERY quiet.

And VERY calm.

"I think I'm doing it!" the house thought.

And she almost was.

But then, the wind came.

RUSTLE

RUSTLE

RUSTLE

It started with a . . .

SCRATCH!

And a gust through her roof let out a

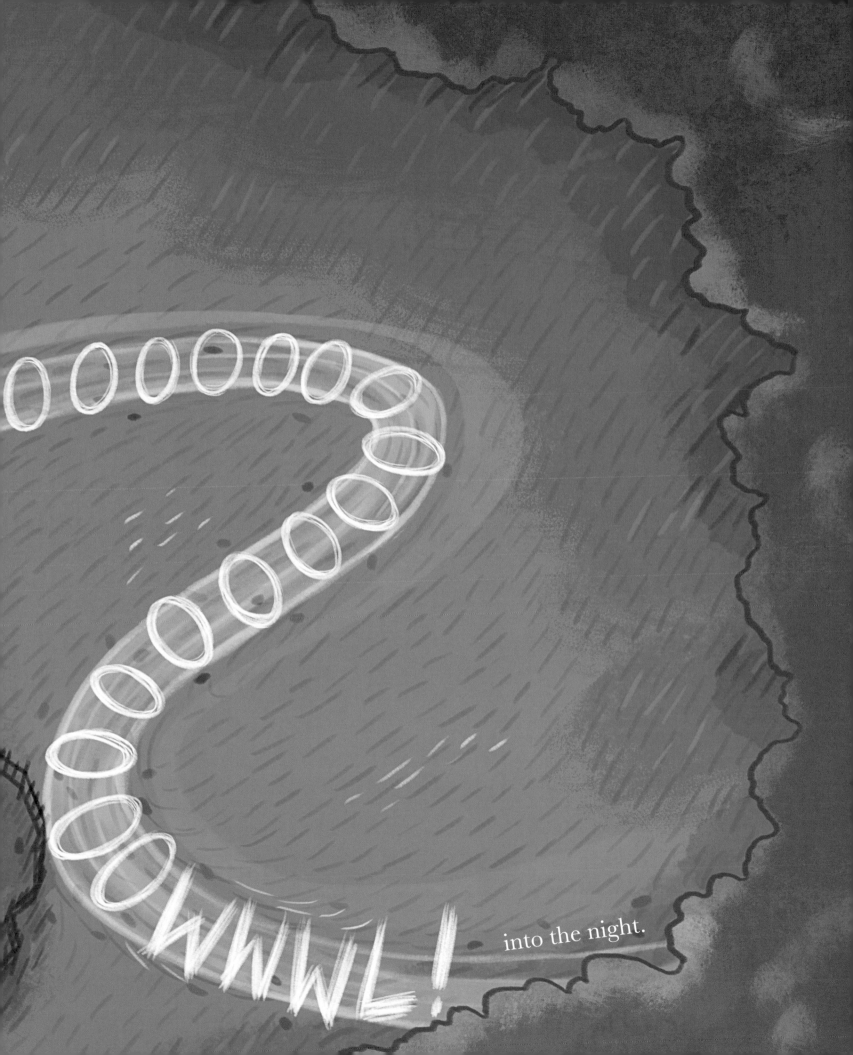

"Whoa," thought the house.

"That was fun."

Once the wind had gone, the night was quiet, still, and calm.

But the house did not have to be.

She liked being noisy.

Maybe she *liked* being haunted.

But that didn't keep the house from feeling lonely.

"I'll just have to find people who like that I'm spooky," she thought.

"A family who will help this haunted *house* become a haunted *home*."

That's when she saw them,
coming up the hill.

They came inside. They made themselves at home.

And that house on that hill was happy . . .

to be

HAUNTED!